MONSTER MAX

AND THE MARMALADE GHOST

ROBIN BENNETT

ILLUSTRATED BY
TOM TINN-DISBURY

Firefly

First published in 2022
by Firefly Press
25 Gabalfa Road, Llandaff North, Cardiff, CF14 2JJ
www.fireflypress.co.uk

Text copyright © Robin Bennett 2022
Illustrations copyright © Tom Tinn-Disbury 2022

A CIP catalogue record of this book is available from the
British Library.

1 3 5 7 9 8 6 4 2

ISBN 9781913102821
ebook ISBN 9781913102838

*This book has been published with the support of the Books
Council of Wales.*

Typeset and designed by
Becka Moor

Printed and bound by CPI Group (UK) Ltd, Croydon,
CR0 4YY

Dedication

To anyone who loves marmalade -
including Paddington
RB

For Zach, my very own Monster Max
T T-D

ALL ABOUT MAX

Max is a very special boy: he can turn himself into a scary monster just by **BURPING**. And he can turn himself back again by **SNEEZING**.

This is because he comes from a land called Krit. Perched on the top of a very pointy mountain, it's the smallest, most hidden country in the world. Also, in Krit, being able to change into a monster, wolf, bear or bat isn't considered unusual at all. For example, Max's mum comes from Krit and she can turn into a wolf.

Sometimes, Max burps by mistake, which can be a nasty surprise if you are standing next to him in the supermarket. And flowers make Max sneeze, so he often finds himself far from home in just his pants.

These days, he's trying to be a better monster ... with mixed results.

He's even got a logo:

1

HELICOPTER STRIKE ... AT NIGHT

Max and his (joint) best friend Peregrine were at Max's house playing MONSTER MAX AND THE MIGHTY PEREGRINE version I.2.

The monitor showed a cold night in dark mountains far, far away from home and the boys were on their deadliest rescue mission yet: Max's parents and his cat, Frankenstein, had been captured and taken to Krit by Fanghorn and his evil Red Eye wolves!

The game had VR and voice control, so it felt completely real. A bit too real, actually...

The boys looked out of their rescue helicopter as it screeched across the starry sky. Then they looked at each other.

'Shouldn't the turny thing on top be going around?' asked Max.

'If you mean the rotor blades? Then, "yes" would be the answer to that question,' said Peregrine. 'Definitely.'

'And should the skinny bit at the back be on fire?'

'No. Most certainly not.'

'Well, I don't think much of your helicopter building,' said Max, as both boys peered down at the dark and very scary forest they were about to crash into. 'I thought you were meant to be a Genius Inventor and All-Round Smarty Pants.'

'I am,' said Peregrine huffily (as huffily as someone who is just about to be squished into the side of a tree can sound). 'But most helicopters aren't designed to have angry Rock Giants throw boulders at them. I can't think of everything.'

'I suppose you'd like me to burp,' said Max.

'That would be useful,' said Peregrine.

'Well, Ohhhh Kayyy,' said Max, making it sound like he was doing Peregrine a massive favour.

So he burped…

There was a flash of light and the VR goggles showed Max the boy double in size and grow several very large teeth and a lot of extra hair, just as he could in real life.

'Roar!' said Max the monster. 'Grat feels great,' he continued through a mouthful of long, pointy teeth. 'At least one of us knows grot he's doing … um, so grot next?'

Peregrine sighed.

'We jump out of this thing,' he replied, 'before we die horribly.'

'Gro Kay!' said Monster Max, grinning from horn to horn … and they jumped.

Monster Max landed with a tremendous THUMP, making the ground shake, sending up huge clouds of snow. The Hero Jump, he liked to think of it. Then he looked up, scanning the night sky for any sign of Peregrine.

'Aaaaarrrrggghhh!' said Peregrine, as he fell out of the swirling black clouds.

'Grotcha!' said Max, catching Peregrine easily. Unfortunately, claws don't work very well on wet rocks and his long, spiky talons, which he was using to grip the shiny, smooth ground, started to slip.

This would've been fine had it not been for the cliff – the great big cliff, right in front of them.

'Weeee!' said Monster Max.

'I don't think so,' muttered Peregrine, as two large grabbers sprang out of his backpack and gripped onto a handy tree.

They stopped falling, but a deep roar (that wasn't Max) echoed from the craggy rocks above their heads. A very large tree flew into the air.

'The Rock Giants are still chucking things at us!' shouted Peregrine as the tree hurtled towards them, its roots and branches shaking in the moonlight.

It landed on Peregrine's metal grabbers with a horrible crunching noise, instantly smashing them to pieces. Both boys started falling down the cliff again.

The Rock Giant's large, stony head looked over the edge as they tumbled into the darkness and it waved its fists.

Max wrapped himself into a big furry ball around Peregrine, to protect him from any more flying trees and from whatever they were going to hit when they landed.

'Ooof, ow, oooof,' (more rocks), 'ow, ow ow, ouch, OOOFFF!' Max added as they finally came to a stop. 'You algright, Grerigrine?'

'Yes, I suppose.' Peregrine looked a little pale but fine.

Up ahead, in the distance, looking like a very large needle, was their destination: the mysterious mountain of Krit.

'We still have to get up there and rescue your parents from Fanghorn,' said Peregrine. He glanced at the timer on his Fanghorn Alert Radar Tracker (FART). 'We've only got two minutes and thirty-seven seconds before Fanghorn and the rest of the Red Eye wolves make them into dinner.'

'Grat Fanghorn is grorrible,' said Max. 'I think it's time to get out of here.'

'Quite.' Peregrine pressed a button on the badge of the school blazer he wore even on Saturdays. Instantly Peregrine inflated, like a giant beachball with a tiny head. He started to float up.

'Hold onto my legs!' he shouted at Max.

They soared over the Rock Giant's surprised head.

After a few minutes of holding onto Peregrine's incredibly shiny shoes, Max (who wasn't too fond of heights) finally plucked up the courage to open one eye in his VR goggles. He gasped.

Krit!

Thin, streaky clouds parted to uncover the moon. It lit up the top of the mountain and the tiny and mysterious Kingdom of Krit: a secret world, hidden by clouds and forests and magic. Home to Ice Witches, Sprites and Shape-shifters. Max's mother's country and also his, he supposed, although he lived in England, near Oxford.

'There's the castle stronghold,' said Peregrine. 'We're going down.'

Fangorns
Castle

Scary
Lake

Clouds
(here be
Monsters)

Sprites &
Oozlums
live
here

Rock Giants

Wolves

Dark Forest

Big hole

KRIT

He started to let the air out of his suit and they drifted towards a tall, fairytale castle by a lake that reflected the stars like a mirror. 'We need to get inside and get to the main tower – that's where your parents and Frankenstein will be,' said Peregrine. 'I'll aim for the courtyard.'

They landed with a bump as Peregrine let the last of the air out of his inflatable clothes.

'I don't think that's regulation school uniform,' said Max.

Before Peregrine could think up a suitably cutting answer, a pair of red eyes lit up in front of them. Hundreds more red eyes blinked on like lasers all pointed in their direction. A howl came from one of the castle battlements followed by the scraping of claws on cobblestones as the ground shook.

'Uh oh,' said Peregrine.

'Yep,' said Max, who was far too scared to burp at the sight of hundreds of evil Red Eye wolves charging towards them.

**GAME OVER ...
YOU LOST ... THANK
YOU FOR PLAYING
MONSTER MAX AND THE
MIGHTY PEREGRINE**

They sat staring at the blank screen. Max had to admit Peregrine had created a great game, but he couldn't see how they would ever get past the wolves, even with Max's monster strength and Peregrine's inventions.

'We're never going to get into the tower. This game's impossible,' he said grumpily.

'We just need to practise,' said Peregrine. 'One day we might have to do this for real and we need to be ready.'

Max groaned: practise = boring in his view.

Just then, Max's cat and (joint) best friend, Frankenstein, strolled into the library of Max's strange and unusual house, which was ordinary on the outside and huge on the inside. The library was where the boys had recently set up their Centre of Operations for 'Protecting and Doing Good Stuff'.

The cat yawned.

He looked at Max, then at Peregrine. Then he yawned again, as if making a point.

'Let's go out,' said Max.

2

THE TOOT BALDEN DAY CENTRE FOR OLD (AND NOT SO OLD) PEOPLE

Going on patrol was something the boys did at least once a day. Frankenstein always came, too – usually in the hope that Protecting and Doing Good Stuff would lead to other things like Eating Slimy Leftovers From Bins and Chasing Ducks.

It never did, so Frankenstein usually wandered off after a bit. The boys left him climbing a tree in the park, with some scruffy-looking pigeons watching him carefully from a branch.

'Let's try some of the quieter streets,' suggested Peregrine.

'OK,' said Max.

If he was honest, he was feeling nearly as bored as his cat. Since they had captured the Grimp and sent it back to Max's home country of Krit, very little had happened, and now the summer holidays that he'd been really looking forward to didn't seem quite so exciting.

However, as they were going past a bunch of bins near the park, Max's monster senses picked something up. (This sometimes happened, even when he was just Max, the boy.)

Peregrine looked at him. 'What is it?'

'Hmm, dunno.' Max looked

around. 'It's weird. Can't see anything dangerous...'

The quiet street curled around a corner leading to a neat set of bungalows next to the Toot Balden Day Centre for Old (and not so old) People.

Outside one of the red-brick bungalows, there was a smartly-dressed old man wearing a dark green hat. He had several shopping bags on the pavement around him. He looked worried and was muttering to himself, which made his moustache go up and down like a speckly, grey caterpillar.

'Why, hello, elderly person,' said Peregrine (who was terrible with old people). 'How may we rescue you from your dilemma?'

The old man jumped as if he'd only just noticed them. This was mainly because he'd only just noticed them.

'Didn't see you there – blind as a mole with the wrong spectacles.' He paused as he played back what Peregrine had just said. 'What's that about rescuing my llama?'

'He's asking if we can help,' said Max, who spent a lot of time with Peregrine and was beginning to figure out how he spoke.

'Oh!' The old fellow beamed at the boys and his eyes went scrunchy. Max decided he was nice. 'That's very kind. Well, I've been extremely foolish and I left my house to go shopping but forgot my keys and now the door's locked behind me.' (At this point Max started to look for somewhere to burp where he wouldn't be seen.) 'I'd ring my daughter who has a spare set but she's on holiday … and there's a sponge cake in the oven…'

From behind a big bush, there came a big burp and a flash.

'Grummy!' said someone big and hairy.

'Weren't there two of you just a second ago?' said the nice old man.

'Yes.' Peregrine thought quickly. 'My

friend Max has gone to fetch a fireman,' he said. 'A surprisingly hairy fireman,' he added, as Monster Max stepped out from behind the bush.

'Ta da! Quick as a flash,' said Monster Max. 'Grello.'

'By golly, yes, that was quick. Well, young fireman…' The old man peered up at Max. 'How can I thank you? Oh, and my name's Reg, by the way. I hope you can get the door open without having to smash it down … but I'm sure you know what you're doing,' he added politely.

'Grat's right,' said Max, who was actually wondering how to pull the door off its hinges without breaking it.

However, he needn't have worried: as he turned, he saw Peregrine slide what looked like a long silver pen back into the top pocket of his blazer, alongside all the real pens he kept there.

'Easy,' said Peregrine, smiling a rare smile. 'I just used my Door Open Real Kwik device.' He pushed the door open.

'DORK,' said Monster Max under his breath.

'What was that?' said Peregrine.

'Nuffink.'

'Why, that's marvellous!' Reg paused, as if something had just occurred to him. 'But why did we need a fireman?'

'To carry the shopping,' said Peregrine, grinning at his friend. He held the door back to let Reg go past and into the bungalow. 'Cake, you say?'

Half an hour later, Max and Peregrine were drinking cups of tea in a cosy living room full of photographs and little ornaments. Max, who had gone into the downstairs loo and sneezed once he'd put all the bags in the kitchen, was on his second slice of cake and enjoying himself immensely.

Reg was full of interesting stories. He'd been a professional cricketer and had been quite famous ('Ooh, a very long time ago, before your parents were born, probably!') and he had travelled the world and had even lived in Australia.

'Well, I came back to where I was born, eventually... I'm on my own now, of course.' He looked sad for a moment, then smiled. 'Can't complain, though, boys. I've got lots of friends at the day centre – and two new ones now!' He slapped his leg. 'Tell you what, why don't you come and meet some of them tomorrow, if you're not too busy? We always go to the day centre on Wednesday mornings. You might find it dull; we just natter, play cards and a bit of chess … but there's always something nice for afternoon tea.'

Max looked at Peregrine. Max knew his friend loved to play chess but, mainly, they were both thinking the same thing – there was bound to be something useful they could do with all those old people about.

Even if it was just helping them finish the cake.

'Well, that went well,' said Peregrine as they wandered home, after they had said goodbye to Reg and thanked him for tea.

'Hmm,' said Max.

'You're not still annoyed about me making you carry all the shopping bags?'

'Nope,' said Max (who was a bit). But mainly he was wondering if they would get something more interesting to do than carrying shopping bags – you didn't need to be a monster for that.

At that moment, the hair stood up on the back of his neck again, just as they passed the same bins as before. He still couldn't see anything obviously dangerous, so he shrugged and they turned to cut across the park.

'It's probably nothing,' he said to no one in particular. But it was a bit weird: his Monster Danger Sense didn't normally make mistakes.

Behind the boys' backs, a lid lifted on a wheelie bin at the corner of the street. A pair of black eyes blinked in the darkness, watching as Max and Peregrine headed home.

'Gotcha!' rasped a scratchy voice, as long, bony fingers stroked a long, bony chin.

PHANTOM POOS

Two weeks earlier ... deep in the forests at the tippie-most top of Krit, Fanghorn, leader of the Red Eye wolves, spoke to the Wight with the mysterious brown bag who stood in front of him.

'So, Wight, you have brought your Bag O'Spooks to me?'

'Well, here I am, right? And I've got this big sack with me.' The Wight, who was about three feet tall, grinned at Fanghorn, all long, pointy chin and green eyes. 'And I ain't Father

Christmas, am I?'

Fanghorn leaned closer to the Wight, showing his razor-sharp, bone-white teeth, breathing hot wolf breath on his face.

'Pooh!' said the Wight. 'When did you last brush your teeth?'

Fanghorn growled. This Wight was very annoying – he didn't seem scared of him at all. Normally Fanghorn would just eat the Wight, but he looked old and very bony, plus he needed him … well, he needed the ghosts the Wight had trapped in his magic sack. He glared instead, and licked his lips for good measure.

'So, thirty gold pieces now and you go to England and release the spirits near their home.'

'And thirty more when the job's done, mate,' said the Wight cheekily.

'Yes,' said Fanghorn. 'They will cause panic and great fear and the princess will have to come back to Krit to get help to rid her new country, this England, of them.'

'That's the plan, Boss,' said the Wight. 'These ghosts are top-notch, A1, quality phantoms from some of the most haunted and terrifying places on the planet. Never let me down.'

'Good, we will capture her as soon as she arrives. Princess or not, she is mine. Here!'

Fanghorn tossed a heavy purse in the Wight's direction with his teeth.

'And there's one other thing,' he said, as the Wight snatched up the gold and made to leave with his mysterious sack.

'Wossat, then?'

'She has a son…'

'Oh, yeah?'

'…I want him, too.'

Luckily, Peregrine and Max were completely unaware of all these terrible goings-on (in Krit and in nearby bins) as they made their way the next morning to the day centre. Max had persuaded Frankenstein to come too.

'Retired people like cats,' he explained, 'probably even you.'

As they walked through the double doors, they were met by Reg and a horrible gurgling, belching, farty noise.

'That's not me,' said Reg cheerfully. 'We've been having some problems with the plumbing this morning. Mrs Dempsey dropped her false teeth down the toilet when she sneezed and since then the whole system seems to have a mind of its own!'

Max and Peregrine exchanged a look.

They'd been right – there was probably loads of stuff they could do to help around here.

'Ooh, what a beautiful-looking cat!' exclaimed Reg, looking down.

(Yes, thought Max, Reg really does need better glasses.)

Reg tickled Frankenstein behind the ear and he started to purr like an old chainsaw (the cat, not Reg).

'The residents would love to meet him,' said Reg.

So Max and Peregrine left Frankenstein with Reg and went to investigate the toilets. It didn't need Max's monster ears, or his monster nose, to figure out where the problem was.

'Urgh!' said Peregrine, looking a bit sick as he stared into the cubicle. 'I'm glad I didn't eat much for breakfast.'

'I did,' said Max unhappily.

Max had once seen a documentary in Geography about volcanic mud-pools: he had spent a happy hour in class looking at different types of mud bubbling up, making sloppy, burpy noises. The whole class had loved it (except Kenneth). Looking at what was coming up out of the loo and several basins in the toilets reminded him of the documentary.

In a bad way.

'What do we do?' he asked Peregrine.

'Don't ask me,' said his friend. 'They're going to need a plumber. Possibly several… What?'

Max was staring very hard at something behind Peregrine. He's seen something spooky or dangerous and he's going to turn into a monster, thought Peregrine. And sure enough, Max burped and there was a flash of blue-white light.

'Er, Grerigrine?' said Monster Max. 'I think you should gret out of here.'

Peregrine looked deep into Max's large monster eyes and saw the reflection of something lumpy and horrible rising up out of the loo, like a half-formed creature and he knew this wasn't the usual sort of toilet problem. There was something going on … Krit stuff. And Max, (being from Krit) was going to have to deal with it.

'OK,' he said, not daring to turn around. 'I'll just wait outside the door … you know, stop anyone coming in.'

'Grighty ho,' said Monster Max. 'This is going to be grorrible.'

Keeping guard by the door, Peregrine did his best to ignore the disgusting noises coming from the toilets. After a few minutes, they seemed to die down and he was just about to go back in, to check on his friend, when they started up again. Only worse this time.

Eventually the muffled roars and gloopy bellows stopped. Peregrine opened the door a crack and chucked one of his special pepper grenades into the room. There was the bang of a pepper bomb.

'Achoo! Thanks,' said Max, coming out. 'All done,' he said. 'Let us never speak of this again.'

'Um, you've got…' Peregrine sort of half pointed at Max's face.

'What?'

'…bit of … um, toilet paper-thingy on your … yes, that's it … chin.'

'All gone?'

'Thankfully, yes. Here are your spare

clothes,' said Peregrine. Sometimes he felt like Max's mum.

Later, they were being introduced to the residents as if they were heroes.

'Boys! This is Miss Parks,' announced Reg, proudly, as if he had invented her. 'Now, she always sits next to Mrs Patel – they're best of friends.'

'Hello!' they both trilled.

'And this is Sydney.'

'I normally like marmalade,' said Sydney, for no apparent reason. 'Look forward to it.'

'Me too,' said Max supportively.

'And this is Mrs Mwangi, who's playing bridge with Dottie Dempsey … the one who lost her false teeth,' Reg stage-whispered.

'Oh, I heard what you did to fix our toilets!' Mrs Mwangi cried. 'Such clever, good boys – a credit to your families!'

'I don't know,' said Peregrine. He pointed at Max. 'This one can be a bit of a monster.'

'Shank goo,' said Mrs Dempsey, which Max thought was actually quite accurate in the circumstances.

'Marmalade shouldn't do that,' persevered Sydney. 'Like it's got a mind of its own.'

'And last but not least,' Reg carried on, ignoring him, 'is the kind Svenka, our amazing helper. We old folk generally look after everything ourselves but it's always nice to have an extra pair of hands – sadly, not for long: Svenka is only here during her summer holidays, staying with her aunt, before she flies home. Anyway, she's even more charming today because she seems to be carrying a large plate of biscuits and chocolate-chip brownies.'

Svenka had cool hair, her grey eyes reminded Max of his mother and she looked a year or two older than Max. He hoped he didn't have any more bits of toilet paper stuck to his chin.

'Thanks to you boths,' Svenka said seriously. 'I was very worried when the pipes went crazy mad – no money for plumbers ... always no money...' She sighed, then smiled. 'But we have biscuits – boys always love biscuits – especially hero boys!'

'Actually,' said Max, looking at the plate sadly, 'I think I'm a bit full.'

THINGS JUST KEEP GETTING WEIRDER

With the promise of more things that needed doing, the boys went around to the day centre the next day after breakfast to help out. After the very strange toilet problem that he was still trying not to think about, Max had decided to keep an eye on the place.

'For, you know, Krit stuff,' he said to Peregrine. 'There's something going on.'

'What?' Peregrine polished his glasses and looked thoughtful.

'I'm not sure.'

Frankenstein was keen to come too.

'Less showing off this time,' Max told him.

Frankenstein gave him a look, as if to say, 'Look who's talking.'

It still didn't feel very heroic or monstery just helping out at the old people's day centre, but it seemed to make his parents happy.

'I think that's really great. The old folks run the place themselves and have a committee, but I know volunteers are always welcome,' said his mother enthusiastically. 'And it's better than you two being cooped up in that library all day.'

'Hey!' said his dad, who loved spending all day in the library (when he wasn't investigating clouds in far-away places).

He turned to Max and Peregrine. 'Don't forget to bring me back some biscuits, will you?'

When they walked into the reception area, they found Svenka on her phone, a worry line across her forehead.

'Phoning ambulance,' she said, holding the mobile away from her ear. 'Something wrong with Reg.'

'What?' asked Max.

'Or maybe, I should phone fireman … even polices?'

What could possibly be the matter with Reg that he would need all three emergency services?

'He's not on fire, is he?' Peregrine asked.

'No, he's on ceiling.'

'Oh, hello, boys,' said Reg's voice as they walked into the day room. Max and Peregrine looked up.

Something very strange was going on. Max could just about imagine how someone might get stuck to a ceiling (superglue + trampolines ... or one of Peregrine's inventions gone wrong) but that wasn't it...

'You're upside down,' remarked Peregrine (who never missed an opportunity to point out something obvious). 'And you're on the ceiling.' (See?)

'Look, I can walk about up here,' said Reg, strolling past a light fitting.

'Can you come down?' asked Max.

'Unfortunately not,' said Reg, 'but I can do this, look!' And with that, he walked straight through a wall.

Just like that.

'Miaow!' exclaimed Frankenstein, all his hair standing on end as if he'd been struck by lightning.

'MIAOW!' he repeated, but much louder, as Reg walked back into the room, eating a sandwich.

This was too much for Max's cat, who shot out of the room in a streak of sticky-up fur. Through the window, Max saw a Frankenstein-shaped hole in the hedge.

'Is not lunchtime,' said Svenka sternly

to Reg and his sandwich.

Just then Mrs Parks and Mrs Patel came in.

'Ladies,' said Reg, 'you're looking absolutely...'

'...see-through,' Svenka finished for him.

And they were. Max and Peregrine could clearly see what was on the television through their bodies.

Sydney was on the television.

'Help,' he said, looking very unhappy, 'I'm stuck in the telly.' At least he'd stopped going on about the marmalade.

'Whatever you do, don't turn him off,' said Peregrine, which actually sounded like a good idea to Max.

'Hello, boys!'

'AARGH!' said Max. 'Where's your head, Mrs Mwangi?'

'Ish here,' said Dottie, floating up through the floor, carrying Mrs Mwangi's head on a big plate with the lunchtime sandwiches.

'This is terrible,' said Svenka.

I will not turn into a monster, I will not turn into a monster, I will not turn into a monster, I will not turn into a monster… thought Max, who really wanted to turn into a monster. Things were somehow always much less scary when he was scary.

'Max... Max! Stop mumbling to yourself.'

'What?'

'We've got to get out of here,' Peregrine yelled.

'Yes, let's... What about Svenka?'

'She can come with us.'

'No, I stay here – something spooky going on.'

'Oh, really, you think so?' said Max.

'They can't be let out,' said Svenka, ignoring the sarcasm. 'Imagines if they went to supermarket. Old people always go to supermarket.'

'OK, so what's the plan, Peregrine?' asked Max.

Peregrine looked as if he was

concentrating. Finally, he said, 'No idea, let's just get out of here and we can make a plan later.'

'Great plan, let's go!'

Half an hour later – a bit out of breath – they were sitting in the kitchen at home. There was still no sign of Frankenstein.

Max's dad came in. 'Oh, hello – nothing going on at the day centre?'

'Well…' said Peregrine.

'It's gone bonkers,' finished Max, although, if he was honest, he felt that things had suddenly got a lot more interesting. 'Bonkers as in loopy, bananas, cattywumpus, bumfuzzle, gardyloo…'

'All the residents seem to be possessed, flying about, walking through walls,' said Peregrine.

'Stealing sandwiches,' added Max, who felt this was important.

'I wondered if something like this would happen sooner or later,' said his mother, who came in wearing a wetsuit and a bright-red helmet with a light on top.

They all turned and stared at her.

'Wednesday,' she said, as if that explained everything. When they still looked confused, she sighed. 'Underwater caving.'

'OK. Wondered what, exactly, Mum?'

'Well, Fanghorn, leader of the Red Eye wolves, may have worked out that I'm here.'

'He's my arch enemy,' cut in Max's dad, happily.

'We know,' said Max.

'And he's still trying to find me … and maybe you now, Max,' said Mum.

'Uh oh,' said Max.

'OK,' said Max's dad. 'So tell us everything you saw.'

Fifteen minutes later, Max and Peregrine finished telling Max's parents what had happened at the day centre over the past couple of days. Max sensibly left out some of the more revolting details about what went on in the toilets.

There was a short silence. Max's mum looked at Max's dad. Max's dad looked at Max's mum.

'Well, I'm not completely sure, but it sounds like we've got a Ghost Wight on our hands?' said Max's dad.

Max's mum nodded. 'Yes, it does.' She turned to the boys. 'And Wights are sneakier than a fox with a diploma in Sneakology. So he won't be at the day centre, but nearby, so he can control the ghosts but stay out of sight.'

Max remembered the feeling he had when they had passed the bins, like something hidden was watching them – something from Krit.

'I'll help if you need me to,' she added.

'No, that's fine,' said Max quickly.

Finally something interesting was happening – something he could get his teeth into. He and Peregrine could handle it, he was sure. No more computer games for a while, he thought.

Mum nodded. 'OK, but I'll be watching … and you need to sort the ghosts out first, then the Wight.'

'But what do they actually do, these Wights?' asked Peregrine.

Dad cleared his throat. 'Anything for gold, but their speciality is catching ghosts, then using them to cause trouble. You can cause a lot of that if you've got a bag full of ghosts at your command. But Fanghorn is definitely behind this and he's attacking the old people because he thinks they're an easy target…'

'We've got to help them: To Protect and Do Good Stuff!' Max had been dying to say this for ages.

'We need to do some planning, then,' said Peregrine, looking delighted, too.

'Oh no,' said Max.

BATTLE WITH GHOSTS

As soon as they got to the library (Centre of Operations), Peregrine climbed up a step ladder and started scanning the shelves.

'Ah, ha!' he said, removing bits of dead flies and other dried-up insects from a large, canary-yellow book. '*Ghosts in the Machine; the Physics of Phantoms,*' he read from the cover as he climbed down. 'I'm off home. This should be handy when I come to recalibrating my

Personal Animal Nano Tracking Sonar.'

'Just to be clear, then,' said Max, 'you're going home to change your PANTS?'

'How old are you?' Peregrine stared down his thin nose at Max. But he didn't bother waiting for an answer. 'Here,' he said, shoving a familiar book into Max's hands. 'This is more your style – it's got plenty of pictures and I'm sure there are several fart jokes.'

'Ah, yes,' said Max, taking the book and polishing the worn, red leather with the sleeve of his hoodie. '*Kritters of Krit*, my old favourite.'

'I'll be back after lunch. I think that's long enough to leave poor Svenka on her own with all those spooks and spirits. In the meantime, you have to find out as much about Wights as possible. Got that?'

'Yup, leave it with me,' said Max.

Just as he said, Peregrine rang the doorbell a couple of hours later. It woke Max up.

'We really should get you a key,' said Max, yawning.

Peregrine narrowed his eyes. 'Have you been asleep?'

'No, um, yes … a bit – just to keep my strength up. I felt a bit tired after lunch.'

'And how's the research into Wights going?'

'Brilliant,' fibbed Max. 'I have all I need to know at my fingertips!'

'OK, so how do we deal with him/her/they/it?'

'Well…' Max put on his intelligent face, while trying to remember anything he had read before he got hungry, which was before he got sleepy, which was almost nothing. 'We defeat him if we get rid of the ghosts – easy-peasy.'

He was pretty sure it must be something like that, anyway.

'Oh-Kay,' said Peregrine, looking unsure.

'What have you been up to?' Max thought this was a very good time to stop talking about what Max should have been doing – and Peregrine always loved talking about his inventions.

'Well,' his brainy friend said, looking extremely pleased with himself, 'I've made some ghost-vision goggles. According to the book, *Ghosts in the Machine*, all phantoms and spirits give off tons of electricity, so I switched the infra-red sensors on my goggles to magnets and now we should be able to see the ghosts. It's very interesting, in fact, and very similar to the theory...'

'Brilliant!' interrupted Max, pushing Peregrine into the street and slamming the door behind him. 'Let's go!'

When they got to the day centre, someone (Svenka, hopefully) had pushed a heavy table against the double doors so no one could get in. Or out. Even through the double doors, the boys could hear smashing plates and crashing pans from the kitchen.

'Let's go round the back,' suggested Peregrine, who had taken off his PANTS to walk across the park earlier – putting the tracking device in a big rucksack, 'and you might want to...'

'Oh, yes.' Max burped once they were around the corner, out of sight. There was a flash of blue-white light. 'Roar,' he said, 'roar, roar, roary roar.' It was always good to get into character.

'Good. OK, I think we might want to explain things to Svenka first. Let me do the talking; you stay out of the way.'

'Hello, Svenka,' said Peregrine as casually as possible, sliding open the doors at the back of the day centre.

'Thanks Gods you're here. Why's there great big man in fancy dress behind tree?'

'Oh, ah ... that's just Max! He's in a costume and he's on stilts ... and we've got a plan. Come in, Max, don't be shy, silly. It's only Svenka – she wants to admire your disguise.'

Max stepped out from behind the tree. 'Grello, Svenka.'

'Is good costume,' said Svenka, raising an eyebrow. 'So, tell me great plan.'

'...so it's that simple,' said Peregrine, folding up the piece of paper he had been drawing on. 'Svenka, you guard the door, stop anyone coming in. I'll spot the ghosts with my Personal Animal Nano Tracking Sonar and Max – in his costume with spare Ghost Goggles, so he can see the ghosts, too – will frighten them away.'

'You're sure this will work?' Svenka looked doubtful. Max was thinking the same thing.

'It's all in this book,' said Peregrine, showing both of them the copy of *Ghosts in the Machine*. 'The best way to get rid of spirits and spooks is to scare them back – they're not expecting it.'

'OK,' said Svenka.

'Grockay,' said Max. 'To Grotect

and Do Good Stuff!' he cried, and just in time because the kitchen doors suddenly burst open and Sydney (still inside the television, which was on wheels) shot out.

'I'm stuck in here and I haven't even had me breakfast yet,' he said unhappily as he sailed past.

'Hello, boys!' Mrs Mwangi was at least carrying her own head now. Dottie seemed to be having a problem floating at the right height: only the top half of her body was sticking out of the floor.

'There they are!' cried Peregrine. 'Put my spare PANTS on your head, Max!'

Max was amazed how well Peregrine's Ghost Goggles worked. Hovering above the two ladies, Max could now see a creature like a fat spider with threads, like dozens of puppet strings, attached to its many feet. Mrs Mwangi and Dottie were caught in the threads.

Max flicked out a claw as sharp as a brand-new knife and cut the threads. Instantly Mrs Mwangi's head was back on her shoulders and Dottie was standing on the floor.

The spider creature turned to Max and waved its feet threateningly, but Max just grinned with his huge monster teeth and licked his lips. The ghostly spider very sensibly ran off.

Max was wondering what to do about Sydney, who was surrounded by waves of blue-and-red light, like prison bars, when Mrs Parks and Mrs Patel appeared out of nowhere.

With Peregrine's Ghost Goggles, Max understood why they were so see-through: two creatures, looking like goblins in storybooks, were holding a sort of screen in front of them, like a sheet. Max tried grabbing it, but his hands just went through thin air.

'Try something else,' said Peregrine, a bit unhelpfully.

'Everything OK?' shouted Svenka, from her place guarding the door.

Hmm, thought Max and he took a deep breath and blew. The force of the monster breath made Peregrine fall over, but it did the trick. When Max opened his eyes, the magic sheet and the goblins were gone. Mrs Parks and Mrs Patel were looking nice and solid again.

'Anything you can do to help?' asked Reg, appearing through a wall. 'All this walking about on the ceiling is making me feel funny.'

It was easy to see what the problem was. Two ghostly squids had attached themselves to Reg's feet and were gripping the ceiling with powerful suckers.

'I've got this,' said Peregrine, who had picked himself up off the floor. From his pocket, he took a whistle and blew on it.

'Aargh!' said Max, clutching his sensitive monster ears.

'Sorry,' said Peregrine. 'Anti-dog whistle – squids hate loud noise.'

'Clever,' said Monster Max, catching Reg as he tumbled off the ceiling. There was no sign of the ghost squids, who must have slithered off.

'Just Sydney left now!'

Max had no idea what the bands of light were around the television, but they had trapped Sydney inside. Without thinking about the danger, he stretched out his great hairy monster arms and grabbed at the waving lights. Max felt an enormous electric shock go through his whole body, but he didn't let go: he clenched his big monster teeth, flexed his huge monster muscles and held on.

'ROAR!' he roared. 'ROAR!!'

The ghostly electrical energy tried to fight back, like a huge coiled snake, but Max was very strong and determined. He tightened his grip and squeezed even harder.

Electricity flew around the room like tentacles, trying to grab onto everything and anything it could: mirrors were smashed, curtains came off the wall.

Peregrine dived for cover behind a sofa and still Max squeezed, still Max roared … until slowly, bit by bit, the tentacles got weaker and smaller and smaller and … disappeared.

POP!

And just like that Sydney was out of the TV and sitting on the floor, looking with surprise at the big orange monster in front of him.

'Thank you, Mr Wookie,' he said.

Monster Max leaned against the wall, exhausted.

'Big mess,' said Svenka, coming in, 'is over?'

'Yes,' said Peregrine. 'Well done, Max.'

DON'T CELEBRATE TOO SOON

'And a very good morning indeed to you, Madame Pinky-Ponky,' said Peregrine to the housekeeper who was more like a granny to Max.

'Well, 'ello, Master Peregrine, you are just in time for breakfast!'

'Great!'

'Max cooked it.'

'A bit less great!' said Peregrine, following her down the long hallway, past suits of armour, portraits of people looking as if there was a funny smell coming from somewhere, a giant brass pot and Max's mum's extreme dodgeball crossbow.

He spent most days during the holidays over at Max's house, but he still hadn't visited every room or figured out how they managed to fit so many in what seemed such an ordinary house. Over the summer, they had been practising cricket in the ballroom.

'Ah, young Master Peregrine,' said Max's dad over the top of his local paper, which Peregrine was very pleased to see had nothing about the Toot Balden Old Folks' Day Centre being inexplicably haunted.

'Hello, Peregrine,' said Max's mum, smiling. 'I've just made some blueberry and banana smoothies, do you want one?'

'I'm sure he does,' said Max, who was wearing a very tall chef's hat and one of Madame Pinky-Ponky's bright-purple, frilly aprons. He grinned at his friend.

Max had been very tired after all that monstering and madness yesterday but he'd had a long steam bath in the hammam and an early night and now he was feeling great.

'Bacon? Eggs?'

'Yes, please,' replied Peregrine, 'we'll need all our strength for the big clean-up. I assume Max has told you everything?'

'Several times,' said Max's dad. 'Brilliant job converting the tracker. Did you get them all?'

'Course I did,' said Max, looking hurt.

'And the Wight?' asked Max's mum.

'No sign of him,' said Max confidently.

'Must have run off when he saw me waving my claws about.'

Max's mum didn't look so sure.

They arrived at the day centre on the dot of 9 a.m., when it opened.

Svenka was there with Reg. Reg smiled at them, but Max could see Svenka looked tired ... and a bit worried.

'Thanks for yesterday,' she said. 'And today,' she added, handing them a broom and a dustbin bag each.

'Yes, great job sorting out ... well, whatever that was. I've still no idea, really,' Reg said. 'Mind you, I don't know how we're going to pay for all the damages – little money, lots broken. Not your fault!' he added quickly. 'We're very grateful. Good job, you three.'

Max and Peregrine spent all morning helping Svenka clean up. After a quick lunch, they were able to open up the day room to the regulars like Dottie, Sydney and Reg.

They had a celebratory cup of tea and Reg made a speech thanking the boys and Svenka.

'I've seen lots of strange things on my travels, but that tops it all,' he finished.

'In India, they say spirits visit this world when they get bored and want to create mischief,' Mrs Patel chipped in.

'Sorry for no biscuits,' said Svenka.

'That's OK,' both the boys said politely.

'And it's all looking a lot cleaner now.' Mrs Mwangi beamed at them.

'Well! I'm just glad it's all over,' exclaimed Mrs Parks.

'Yesh,' said Dottie, who was still missing her false teeth.

'Yup, all over, all sorted,' said Max confidently.

'Marmalade's still acting funny,' said Sydney, but no one heard him because the residents were busy clapping Max and Peregrine. Max grinned from ear to ear, but Peregrine was looking thoughtful.

Walking back to Max's house a bit later, they were delighted to find Frankenstein waiting for them on the doorstep.

'Where have you been?' asked Max, picking him up.

Frankenstein squirmed in Max's arms and said, 'Miaow,' in a way that could have meant 'nowhere much, hiding up a tree' or 'I was here all the time' – who knows with cats.

'Well, it's good to have you back,' said Max, opening the door for them all. 'How about a game of MONSTER MAX AND THE MIGHTY PEREGRINE?' he suggested, turning to Peregrine.

'Um…' Peregrine looked unsure. 'I've almost finished turning your cellar into my new workshop, after your parents said I could, and I've got a few new machines to test.'

Max frowned at his friend. 'Bor-ring!' he said, with a fake yawn. 'What's wrong with you? We deserve a break after all that amazing hero-ing – most of it done by me.'

'Hmm,' said Peregrine, 'you never know when these things will be needed. It's good to be prepared…'

'Come on, just a quick game. You can do all that work stuff later.'

Peregrine sighed and followed Max up to the library.

'I'll let you win, even though my monster powers can beat your nerdy powers any day,' Max said. He turned the machine on and grinned. 'Hurry up!'

Two hours later, they were still playing MONSTER MAX AND THE MIGHTY PEREGRINE, although Peregrine wasn't really into it and Max was still boasting.

'Ha!' he said, dodging a hail of ice boulders and jumping over a charging wolf. 'Keep up, Peregrine! No room in the adventure for losers!'

Peregrine's character fell down a big hole.

'Oh!' said Max, as the game finished. 'One more go.'

'No, I really need to get on with stuff in the cellar…'

Max's face clouded and he looked as if he was about to say something rude to Peregrine, but just then the phone rang.

There was a muffled conversation in the hall and footsteps on the stairs. Max's dad came in.

'It's for you,' he said, pressing the speaker button on the phone.

'Hello, hello ... Max, Peregrine?' It was Svenka, sounding very worried, even a bit scared.

'Yes, it's us,' said Peregrine.

'Come quickly. There's bony man, all horrible and very rude. Also he's made a sticky orange beast from delicious English breakfast food. This is much worse than before... Be quicks!'

7

THE MARMALADE GHOST

Max felt a cold trickle, like water, run down his spine. It could have been guilt and the first suspicion that perhaps he wasn't such a great monster after all.

'That sounds like the Wight – I thought he was sorted?' his dad asked, looking at Max.

'Me too,' said Peregrine, also looking at Max.

Max did his best to act cool.

'Oh, they sometimes don't know when

they're beaten,' he said, shrugging his shoulders, as if he knew. 'Let's change the subject.'

'Let's go and get ready,' said Peregrine. 'We need to hurry.'

Ten minutes later, Max's dad dropped them off outside the day centre. They needed a lift because of all the kit Peregrine insisted on bringing.

Max's mum had come along and both his parents had asked (several times) if they could help. Both the boys refused and eventually Max's parents had agreed to let the boys go in, but to stay outside, just in case. And look after Frankenstein, who showed no sign at all of wanting to get out of the car.

'Mind you, ideally, I would have

had time to test all this,' Peregrine grumbled. 'If I hadn't been made to play computer games.'

'I'm sure it's fine,' said Max, trying to burp but not doing a very good job of it.

'I haven't even named any of them.'

'I'd say that was a good thing,' said Max. 'Round the back?' he suggested.

Peregrine nodded and started to unzip his massive bag. So far everything was quiet and looked normal, but Max felt the monster hair on the back of his neck stand up and he really couldn't wait to burp.

Svenka must have seen them through the window because she ran out as they came around the corner. From inside the day centre, they heard a horrible gurgling, roaring noise and an even more worrying chuckling noise: high-pitched and scratchy.

'Luckily all old people not here today. They're safe.'

'Can you keep a secret?' asked Max, and he burped before she could answer.

'Ha! I knew it,' said Svenka, looking up at Monster Max, who was grinning at her. 'And after last two days, nothing surprise me anymore.' She looked over at Peregrine. 'Now you turn into big bird or something?'

'No,' said Peregrine, strapping onto his back a very shiny new machine covered in fans and mirrors and with a large net on a catapult. 'I'm the smart one. Here,' he said, rummaging in his bag, bringing out something that looked like a rocket-launcher tube and handing it to Svenka.

'You might find this comes in handy.'

'More plumbing things?'

'No,' said Peregrine. 'Just point the pointy bit at anything you don't like and squeeze the trigger here: it fires very strong glue bombs. Anything it hits will be stuck to the next thing it touches.'

'Is good,' said Svenka. 'Now we go – gooey ghost is getting bigger and horrible little mans...' She shrugged. 'I shall shoot nasty Gollum with fancy drainpipe.'

'To Grotect and Do Good Stuff!' roared Max and, with that, they burst through the doors.

'Who brought the circus?' shouted a hidden voice coming from the top of the curtains. 'Uh oh!'

In a blur, Svenka had brought the

bazooka up to her shoulder and fired. There was a large splat. A grey-black shape scuttled across the ceiling and hid behind some shelves.

It shouted, 'Missed!'

'Only just,' said Svenka, grimly.

'You reload by pulling the handle at the side!' shouted Peregrine. But before she had a chance to fire again, a gloopy 'whoo' noise filled the room and Max's monster hair stood straight on end, as if it'd just been blow-dried.

His monster ears picked up the sound of something glass rolling down the corridor. He waited as a jar with the words 'Mum's Marmalade' on the outside rolled slowly into view.

And stopped.

The lid began to twist open, all by itself

– or by some ghastly, ghostly hand – and the contents flowed out of the open pot.

There was loads of the stuff, glugging and oozing upwards until it was floating in the air: a shuddering blob that slowly took on the shape of a sticky orange creature. Two eyes popped open with two tiny sucking sounds and stared right at Max.

As the shimmering spectre floated across the room, its sheets of sticky stuff wobbled and wavered and dripped on the carpet. With flappy hands and a small open mouth making a woo shape, it was the colour of a dark sunset, filling the room with ghostly noises and a very strong smell of oranges. Deep inside this ghost, something glowed.

'YUM!' said Monster Max.

He leaped forward.

And missed. The Marmalade Ghost was surprisingly quick.

'NOT SO FAST!' Monster Max pounced again, this time grabbing hold of the sticky swathe of tacky marmalade, which immediately wrapped itself around him, like a large roll of clingfilm.

'Help!' said Max's muffled, monstery voice.

Blaht, blaht, went Svenka's bazooka.

'OW,' Monster Max yelled.

'Sorry, got bit excited,' said Svenka.

'Step aside!' Peregrine marched forward, a look of grim determination on his face, and pressed the button on his belt. Like a giant fly swatter, the net behind his back slammed down and covered Max and the Marmalade Ghost.

'Gotcha!' cried Peregrine triumphantly.

'Got me too,' said a still-muffled Monster Max, who wasn't having much fun.

'Don't worry, we'll separate you, when we get this thing sucked up.'

He pressed another button on his belt and the nozzle of a giant hoover shot out. Unfortunately, instead of sucking up all the sugary, possessed marmalade, it started blowing warm air all over the room.

Peregrine frowned. 'Something's wrong,' he muttered and he pressed the button again, but this time the end of the giant vacuum cleaner fell off with a clang and just lay there on the ground like the world's worst snake. The hot air was still blowing from his vacuum pack, and blew Peregrine out of the double doors and into the large conker tree outside.

'WHAT'S GRAPPENING?' asked Max, still wrapped in ghost.

'You're losing, that's what!'

A bony, grey face poked out from behind the shelves, grinning like a walnut with bad teeth. 'You lot are rubbish,' he jeered. 'Never work with children or animals they say. Losers! OK, I'm off – old marmalade chops has got this wrapped up. Ha ha – bye!'

Svenka turned and fired two more glue bombs, but the Wight smashed a hole in the thin ceiling and disappeared.

There was a sort of explosion of orange light and suddenly the room was full of small marmalade balls with

snappy teeth, bouncing around, biting anything that moved.

Max, mainly.

'Grouch ... grouch ... grouch ... ROARRRR!'

The force of the roar hurled the orange balls across the room and ripped the net covering Max to shreds, just as Peregrine burst back onto the scene, bits of tree in his hair. He pressed the net button on his suit again, but unfortunately the wooden arm snapped and the net just went over his head.

The marmalade balls gathered into one big blob that expanded in size until it was larger even than Max.

'Grikey!' he said, as the marmalade turned into a spooky phantom with sticky claws and a huge round mouth.

'Whoooooo!' it howled.

'I think we better get out of here … right now,' said Peregrine.

'Grery good idea!' said Max as he picked up Svenka and ran outside. Then he sneezed, thanks to a handy flowerbed near by.

As he left, Peregrine threw several smoke bombs at the Marmalade Ghost, which kept it back just long enough for them to close all the doors and lock them.

Outside, Max's mum had got out of the car.

'Are you all right?' she asked. 'I was about to come in.'

'Only just,' said Max. 'This is Svenka, by the way. She knows about the monstering and she's cool. Can you give her a lift?'

'Of course! Where do you live?'

'Just there.' Svenka pointed a trembling hand at a small block of flats like the one Reg lived in. 'My aunt's not back until late.'

'Then come home with us,' said Max's mum. 'You can get cleaned up and have something nice to eat. In fact, you all look like you could do with a bath and a rest. What was going on in there? The noises were terrible … and I saw something climbing on the roof. It was getting dark, but I could tell it was from Krit.'

Svenka looked up sharply.

'Back in my country, they tell stories about this Krit… Is real?'

Max was just about to ask what stories, when he noticed Peregrine holding back and frowning.

'Aren't you getting in the car?' he asked his friend.

'No,' said Peregrine. 'I'll walk home, thanks.'

'But,' said Max, 'we've got to plan what we do next.'

Peregrine had been turning away, but now he spun on his heel to face Max, his face white with anger in the gloom.

'Plan? What? You mean look at books and research, like you said you did about the Wight?'

'I, um...' started Max. 'I might not have read everything I could.'

'You mean nothing at all, because the Great Monster Max doesn't need to read books or test his equipment instead of playing stupid games ... or take anything seriously at all in fact, because he's so marvellous, everything will be fine – except it isn't, it wasn't and that's basically your fault! Big, hairy idiot.'

Before Max could say anything, even to agree, Peregrine threw the broken pieces of his equipment on the ground and stormed off into the late-evening darkness.

'Awkwards,' murmured Svenka from the backseat of Max's parents' car.

There was a long pause. Max thought about going after Peregrine, but he felt a bit stupid. And that's because I am, he thought. Stupid.

He couldn't bear to look at Svenka or his parents.

'Come on, Max; let's go home,' said Max's dad gently. 'We'll see what we can do about all this later.'

BAD

The next day, Max lay in bed until 9 a.m. looking at the ceiling, pretending he wasn't waiting for the ring of their front doorbell that meant Peregrine was just in time for breakfast as usual.

But Peregrine didn't come.

Eventually Max went downstairs. His dad was making pancakes with Madame Pinky-Ponky – a sure sign he was trying to cheer someone up. His mum was reading a 'thank you' note from Svenka that had been pushed through the door earlier.

'She also says thanks for trying – to you and Peregrine, too,' Max's mum said to Max, who just said, 'Mm hmm,' because he didn't think he deserved to be thanked for anything.

'Her aunt is making her stay at home today. Svenka writes that she'll keep the ghost and monster thing, "all that crazy cool stuff," she says, "big, scary secret between us." She's told her aunt, who told the council, that the day centre had a food-safety problem.'

'I guess that's partly true,' said Max's dad, but no one laughed.

Frankenstein slinked in and Max, who didn't really feel like eating, gave him a bit of his pancake without his parents seeing. Frankenstein purred quietly and rubbed up against Max's leg. At least you still like me, thought Max.

'I think you should go to Peregrine's house.' His dad put a mug of cocoa in front of Max. 'You can take that bazooka contraption of his that Svenka left. Perhaps it would be a good excuse to patch things up? And you could work out what to do about this Wight.'

Max felt a twinge of guilt, quickly followed by a flash of annoyance. 'I don't need Peregrine,' he said, a bit snappily. 'And, anyway, it's this Marmalade Ghost we need to sort.'

'I think we all know where this trouble is coming from,' said Max's mum, looking serious.

'Fanghorn?' said Madame Pinky-Ponky.

'Yes. Perhaps I should take a trip back to Krit,' Mum said. 'Try and sort all this out.'

'I shall come too,' said Madame Pinky-Ponky, looking fierce and determined – as fierce and determined as anyone four feet tall in non-matching bunny-rabbit slippers can look.

'I'm not sure that's a good idea,' said Dad, but Max didn't hear what his mother had to say about that because he'd heard enough and was already making for the door.

'Gotta go!' he shouted over his shoulder. 'Thanks for breakfast!'

Max marched out of the front door. He had just one thing on his mind: to stop his mum going back to Krit. And that meant he had to sort this thing out on his own, which meant no mums and definitely no nerdy know-all Peregrines. Frankenstein tried to follow him along the road, but Max told him to go home. Frankenstein pretended not to understand. He followed Max all the way to the park, until Max had to say, 'Shoo!' angrily and walk away. He glanced back, just before he crossed the road to the day centre, and saw his (joint/only) best friend standing by the swings, looking hurt.

When Max got to the end of the quiet road which led to the day centre, he stood and watched a man in a green-and-yellow council van get out and nail a sign on the door with the word:

CLOSED!

in big, black lettering. Max would have gone closer to read what the rest of the sign said, but there was a small crowd of people blocking his way.

A small crowd of old people, to be precise.

Max took a deep breath and walked over. Rather slowly.

Mrs Mwangi was the first person he saw but, for once, she wasn't smiling.

'Young man! What have you been doing to our lovely day centre?'

'I, er,' Max started to stutter but he really didn't know what to say next.

'Nothing but trouble since you boys came, everything broken...'

'...and no money for repairs and now people from the council say it is closed for food safety,' added Mrs Patel.

'I told you the marmalade was haunted,' said Sydney.

Mrs Mwangi folded her arms. 'We want a quiet life. We don't want you bad boys around here no more.'

'OK,' said Max, turning to go. 'Um …
sorry, for everything.'

He was nearly at the corner when Reg
caught up with him.

'Don't worry about that, son,' he
said, puffing a bit. 'They're angry, but
they'll calm down and realise the day
centre would probably have had to close
anyway, because of money, and I don't
think any of that … er … stuff really
had anything to do with you or your
friend. Perhaps come around in a few
days for a nice cup of tea?'

'Thanks,' said Max, staring hard at his
shoes. He might have had something
in his eye.

Max walked sadly across the park.
He had planned to go around the

back, turn into a monster and fight the Marmalade Ghost (and win this time!), but he just didn't have the energy – or the confidence.

He saw Frankenstein by some bushes up ahead and felt his spirits lift a bit; they'd go for a walk together and he would figure something out. It was a sunny day, with plenty of families having picnics or playing football and cricket. Everything seeming nice, normal and just what Max was there to protect.

Max was rummaging about in his pocket to see if he had a treat to give his (definitely only) friend when something bony and grey popped out from behind a thorn bush.

And snatched Frankenstein.

LIBRARY

Max blinked several times – very quickly – and tried to compute what had just happened. In fact, when he thought about it, it was very obvious what had just happened: someone (or some thing, more likely) had stolen Frankenstein. Right in front of him, in broad daylight.

Max had never felt scared, confused and really, really angry all at once before. But he did now – and it wasn't nice.

His first thought was to turn into a

monster and charge after whatever had snatched Frankenstein – roaring and smashing things out of his way. But there were far too many families around, enjoying the sunny day, and however furious and frantic Max felt right now, he didn't want to frighten any small children.

Except whatever stole his cat and (only) best friend … he wouldn't have minded a bit of terrifying in their case; even some gobbling up, then spitting out and gobbling up again.

His next thought was what would Peregrine do? But asking him wasn't really an option at the moment.

Instead, he ran home as fast as he could – on human legs – and told his parents.

'Mum, Dad, Mum, Dad, something has stolen Frankenstein!' he said, rushing into the kitchen where they were emptying the dishwasher. 'It's got to have something to do with what's been going on with all the ghosts, I'm sure of it!'

Max stopped and gave a sort of shaky hiccup: a new feeling had just swept through him, like water in his bones.

He was upset.

Seeing the concern on his parents' faces made him realise he was more angry-panicky right now than at any other time in his life. Because everything was going wrong.

His dad understood, and he got up and put his arm around Max's shoulder.

'It's OK,' he said. 'It's OK… We'll sort

something out, I promise.'

'Yes, we will,' said his mother, looking quite fierce and wolf-like. 'Yes, I will,' she added.

'What do you mean?' Max looked up at her, noticing how her eyes always got much greyer when she was thinking about turning into a wolf.

'Things have gone too far and it's up to me to sort this out. All this trouble from Krit. Fanghorn only wants to hurt you to hurt me – because you're my son.'

'I think he wants to hurt me more,' said Max's dad – not unreasonably.

'Probably, which is why I have to leave you both here and go to Krit alone, to face Fanghorn.'

'No!' said both Dad and Max at the same time.

'It's too risky!' said Max.

'To be fair, that's never stopped her,' said his dad.

'But you're always telling me not to take risks.'

'That's because that's our job, as your mum and dad.'

'We're better as a team,' Max tried again.

'Wolves are more dangerous alone,' said his mother.

'Honestly, Mum.' Max was getting desperate for his mum not to go to Krit on her own. 'It's more dangerous for me if I stay here – Dad's cooking is terrible.'

'Madame Pinky-Ponky loves to cook for you,' his mum smiled. 'Don't worry.'

'When has saying "don't worry" ever stopped anyone worrying in the history of the world?'

Max really was beginning to panic. He had to win this argument. His mum going to Krit seemed like a terrible idea.

'Fanghorn's not the only danger in Krit.' He was thinking about Peregrine's computer game they never could win.

'I know. I grew up there. I still have friends.'

'But...' Max searched about for another reason, any reason, that would stop his mother going. He couldn't let her go. He'd messed up, so he had to put it right, that was the rule, but mums weren't good with rules like that, especially if they'd already made up their minds.

Max thought hard.

Really hard.

The computer game popped into his brain again. He was thinking of the part where they always lost, of Fanghorn and his pack in the castle courtyard in the dark: how one pair of red eyes slitted open, like a laser boring into them in the darkness, then another and another until hundreds surrounded them in the courtyard. Max had it!

'Mum, I know why you shouldn't go!'

His mum paused. 'Why?'

'Because it's a trap!' he exclaimed.

There was dead silence in the kitchen. Max's dad looked at his mum and smiled.

'He's got a point,' he said.

So Max's mum reluctantly agreed to stay home. For now.

'Promise,' said Max, 'you're not going to sneak off when my back is turned?'

'I promise,' said his mum. She kissed him on the top of his head and wiggled her little finger. 'Pinky promise.'

'Urgh, Mum, I'm not four!'

But Max was really relieved. 'Thanks, Mum, thanks, Dad. I won't let you down,' he said. 'In fact I won't let anyone down anymore. To Protect and Do Good Stuff and Not Let Anyone Down Anymore!' he cried.

'That motto needs work,' said Max's dad.

'So what are you going to do?' asked his mum.

'What I should have done a long time ago…' said Max, racing up the stairs. He stopped and turned dramatically at the top. 'I'm going to read a book!'

However much he wanted to turn into a monster, roar and smash everything, until the Marmalade Ghost was nothing but splatter and he had his cat back, Max took ten long, deep breaths and forced himself to do what he knew he should have done a long time ago.

He walked into the library and found the very book he was looking for, where he'd left it on the big oak and leather table.

Kritters of Krit

He opened the book and began to read…

The day burned to embers and the moon escaped the group of trees opposite Max's window, slipping through its

tangled cage of branches. As the stars spun and clouds prowled like crouching wolves across the night sky, Max read.

Towers of books piled up around the dim pool of light where he sat. His lips moved silently in time with the words that spun out before his eyes.

He didn't even notice Madame Pinky-Ponky leave a plate of sandwiches and a glass of milk by his elbow.

He'd never read as much in his life: it was like time travel. He read until morning and a pale sun bobbed into the frame of the window like a small, cherry-coloured balloon. Eventually, Max sat back and rubbed his eyes.

He now knew more about his country than he thought possible ... but he still had no idea how to defeat the Wight and get poor Frankenstein back.

He banged his head on the table in frustration and took a deep breath. As he looked up, he read the description of a Wight in *Kritters of Krit* for about the hundredth time.

Are Wights greedy, selfish, untrustworthy, creepy-looking and very, very rude? Certainly. Do they have any good qualities at all? Yes: Wights are very rare, so there aren't many around to spoil your day!

However, some people – mainly other Wights or folk who owe them money – tell you they can be kind if treated in the right way. Unfortunately, no one has worked out how to do this in the last thousand or so years, which was the last time a Wight was known to do anything nice.

Another important thing to know about Wights is that hunters have often laid traps for them because Wights (being greedy) love money. Because they don't trust anyone, they often carry about large quantities of jewels and gold coins, hidden in their many pockets.

Unfortunately they are impossible to catch.

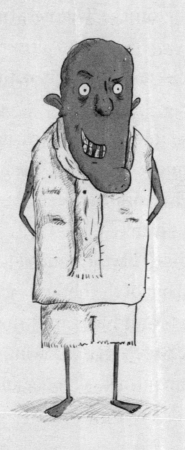

Interesting but not helpful in the least. Max sighed. I've failed, he thought, getting up and going to the window, watching as the sun rose even higher, sparkling on the Thames, turning it from gunmetal grey to a river of ruby, then gold run through with ripples of silver.

He was just about to turn away from the window, when the idea hit him like a firework between the eyes. A plan! His plan!

Max didn't have a moment to lose. He sprinted out of the library, raced down the stairs and burst into the steamy kitchen, which was billowing with the warm, tangy smells of coffee and cooked breakfast.

'Mum!' he shouted at his very surprised-looking mother. 'Have you still got that crown?'

10

ALL WIGHT NOW

Max, carrying a bag that clanked when he put it down, looked up at Peregrine's bedroom window.

'Pssst!' he said, even though it was broad daylight and therefore perfectly all right to ring the bell. Max had the feeling that if he tried the front door, Peregrine would just ask his parents to tell Max he wasn't in. Plus, he was feeling shy – he'd never met either of Peregrine's parents or his little sister.

There was no sign of life at the upstairs window but Max's monster senses told him Peregrine was definitely up there.

'Pssssssttttt!!!' he tried again, but louder.

Still nothing.

Max remembered seeing how someone in a film had attracted the attention of someone upstairs. He bent down and looked for a pebble.

Crash!

Peregrine's angry face appeared at the jagged hole in his window.

'Sorry,' said Max, when Peregrine opened the front door. 'I must have thrown that pebble harder than I thought.'

Peregrine had red spots on his cheeks but otherwise his face was pale and very cross-looking.

'It was more like a rock,' he snapped. 'What did you expect?'

'I…' started Max.

'It wasn't a question and I only came down to tell you that we have nothing to say to each other, except that you owe me fifty quid for a broken window … and here's your rock, in case you want to break any more windows.'

Max swallowed. This wasn't going as well as expected. He had a whole speech prepared but, in the end, he just said, 'The Wight has stolen Frankenstein.'

Peregrine, who had been on the point of closing the door, stopped.

Max took a deep breath. 'And I need

your help to get him back because you're my (joint) best friend and you're really smart.'

Peregrine looked at Max for a few moments. Max held his breath.

'Give me ten minutes,' Peregrine said and then he almost smiled.

Max suddenly felt better than he'd felt in ages.

'Next stop, Svenka,' said Max. Each of the boys was now carrying a large sports bag down the road: they looked very suspicious.

'So you've definitely got a plan?'

'Yup!'

'And this doesn't just involve you turning into a monster and eating everything in sight.'

'Nope, although monstering is involved.'

'And are you going to share this with me at any point?'

'In a minute… Here we are.'

'What are you twos doing?' Svenka was leaning over the tiny balcony of the first-floor flat where she lived with her auntie.

'If you come down, I'll tell you,' said Max.

As the three of them walked to the park, to where the bins were, Max explained his plan and – for probably the first time in his life – Peregrine almost looked impressed.

It was a blustery day with a chilly wind that smelled of rain and felt like the end of summer.

The park was almost empty – and there was no one by the bins, which were a bit whiffy. Max's monster mouth started to water at the thought of all those delicious leftover burgers and ancient sandwiches, but he forced himself to concentrate on the plan.

'OK,' he said to Peregrine and Svenka, 'this is near where Frankenstein went missing and this is also where I keep getting the monster heebie-jeebies every time I walk past.'

'The hibby whats?'

'His hair stands on end whenever there's danger about, or magic, or both,' Peregrine explained to Svenka.

'OK,' she said, 'so Wight hangs out here when not making ghosts to scare old ladies or stealing cats?'

'I'm kind of counting on it,' said Max.

'And these Wights, they really love gold and jewels?'

'Yes,' said Max. 'Ta da!'

He took the crown his mum had leant him out of the bag.

'Wha-?' For once Peregrine was (almost) speechless.

'Is real?' asked Svenka, touching the golden tips of the crown, which sparkled even in the dullness of the day.

'Um, back in Krit, my mum is a princess.'

'And she's trusting you with this?'

'Well, if by trusting you mean she's letting me borrow it on the strict understanding she gets it back, then, yes… And if she doesn't, she'll turn into a wolf and come after the Wight herself and I wouldn't want to be him, if she did.'

'Your friend's family is very strange,' said Svenka, turning to Peregrine.

'You don't know the half of it,' said Peregrine.

Half an hour later, the trap was set. The boys and Svenka watched the crown hanging from the rope, twinkling in the misty rain that trickled down from the grey sky.

'So you know what to do when I turn into a monster?' asked Max.

'Yesssssss, already telling me ten hundred times.'

'And you know what to do when I give the signal, Peregrine?'

Peregrine looked as if he was about

to say something rude to Max, but he stopped and looked alert. 'Did you see that?' he whispered.

The other two peered hard through the gloomy rain. At first, Max could see nothing, but his monster senses were going mad.

Then he spotted it.

It was starting to rain really hard now, but he could just make out a small, grey shape among the shady bits in the bushes.

Slowly, it began to creep out ... towards the glowing crown, which twisted slowly on its rope.

'Have you got your net, Svenka?' whispered Max.

'Yes, is ready.'

'Time to get into position, Peregrine.'

He felt his friend move away as silently as a ninja.

Inch by inch, the creature shuffled forward, its head moving slowly from side to side. It was about three foot high and very bony. One long arm dragged along the ground, the other held something – a cage.

From the bars, a small, untidy tail flicked back and forth.

Frankenstein!

It was everything Max could do not to burp and leap out, roaring his hairy head off, but the Wight was too far away: even with Max's monster speed, it would be gone before he could get close.

'Easy now,' said Max. 'Easy…'

The Wight moved forward, towards the glistening crown …

one cautious step …

half a step …

then a wait, as it sniffed the air like a dog …

another half step …

Max held his breath …

the Wight paused and glared suspiciously right at where they were hiding …

but, then …

it took another step. And that was all that was needed.

'Now!' shouted Max. Svenka leaped forward, bringing the net down with a triumphant cry just as the Wight jumped for the crown, catching it neatly in his spare hand.

And Svenka missed completely.

But the Wight didn't.

For something so old and crabby-looking, he was surprisingly fast. He landed a few feet from Svenka and her net.

Max ran out. 'Give me back my cat!'

'And the nice shiny crown,' added Svenka.

'No, shan't, won't!' snapped The Wight

as he skipped away, grinning. 'You must think I'm as stupid as you two look right now. That crown dangling there – ha ha! Might as well have had a sign in flashing lights saying Big Trap! Especially as this crown is obviously from Krit. Knew it was you and now I'm keeping the crown

and the cat. Might eat it later for me dinner. Yum, yum. Bye bye.'

Max narrowed his eyes. This was it. He burped.

'Roar!' He roared. But not at the Wight. At Svenka. 'Gris is all your fault!'

'Er,' said Svenka, 'so this is scary.'

'You bet is scary!' growled Max, puffing out his chest. He grabbed the useless net in Svenka's hands and threw it right over the tall trees, all the way to the river, then he stomped up to Svenka, breathing monstery breath on her.

'Yeuk!' she said.

Out of the corner of his eye, Max noticed the Wight pause and turn.

'Grr!' Max rumbled. 'Stupid old people, stupid Svenka, can't do anything!'

Svenka cried, 'Oh, please, Mr Big Monster, do not hurt me! I'm sorry I'm so rubbish!'

'Ha! And I love to eat rubbish…'

The Wight had stopped and now took a hesitant step back towards Max and Svenka.

Max pretended not to notice. He roared again. 'Your puny fear just makes me even angrier … and even hungrier, so now I'm going to grobble you all up, even your shoes!'

'Oh, help, help! Who (or even what) is going to save me from this quite hideous monster?'

That did it. The Wight dropped the crown and the cage containing Frankenstein and shot forward.

'Oi! Pick on someone your own size, Toothy!'

'Now!' shouted Max.

Peregrine jumped out from behind his bin and pressed a button on the belt. This time the net worked perfectly. It shot forward and trapped the Wight as Svenka neatly sidestepped Max, picked up the crown and popped it on her head with a big grin.

Max grabbed the cage with Frankenstein in it.

FIGHT BACK

'That's it, never again! A measly thousand years of being really bad and getting horribly rich (an' enjoying meself immensely I might add), then I go and do one teensy, little good deed by trying to save someone being eaten by a monster and I'm banged up for me trouble: captured and chained like a common criminal.'

Max, Peregrine and Svenka glared down at the Wight, who was currently tied to a chair in the cellar. Frankenstein – apparently none the worse for being catnapped – rubbed himself against the Wight's legs and purred. Actually purred. Max rolled his eyes and turned to the Wight.

'That's because you are a common criminal.'

'Steady on. I may be a bit rough around the edges, but I ain't common – I'm what you call a specialist in my field.'

'Stealing cats?'

'Getting ghosts, supplying spirits … purveying poltergeists.'

'OK, if you're the expert,' said Peregrine, 'then help us get rid of this Marmalade Ghost.'

'Nope.'

'What if I did this?' said Peregrine.

'Argh! Is that a water pistol?'

'No,' said Peregrine. 'I've just squirted you with a truth serum and now you're going to tell us how to defeat the Marmalade Ghost.'

'Shan't.'

'More like can't...' Svenka stood in front of the Wight and stared at him. 'Truth serum might not work on wrinkly gnome, but I see truth, ha!'

The Wight looked uncomfortable for the first time. 'What d'yer mean?'

Svenka turned to the other two. 'He's scared: three kids catch him easy. Marmalade Ghost have him for his breakfast. On toasties.'

'I'm not scared,' the Wight spluttered. 'Right, I'll show you. I'll go over to that old folks' place, grab that poxy ghost and I'll…'

He stopped and a cunning look came over his face.

'Wait a minute – you're using that reverse bicycology thingy on me, ain't yer: getting me to do the opposite of what you are saying; trickin' me into 'elping you 'orrible lot. Ha! Nice try but I ain't helpin' no one any more, just gets you into bother – yer on your own. Good luck! You'll need it!'

Max, Peregrine and Svenka looked at each other, wondering what to do next. They were running out of ideas.

Just then, Madame Pinky-Ponky came in with a tray full of tea and raspberry muffins.

'Hello, boys. Hello, Svenka, dearie. Ooh, you've got a friend tied to a chair.

If energy was visible, thought Max, you would have seen an electric-blue line like lightning shoot across the room from Madame Pinky-Ponky straight to the Wight. And back again.

'Little Timmy!' she whispered.

'Valentina!' he croaked back.

Blimey, thought Max, *I always wondered what her first name was.* 'Do you two know each other?'

'We grew up together in Krit. We were best friends.'

'But you left,' said the Wight. 'I looked everywhere for you.'

'I came here. I couldn't leave the princess, and then she had a baby. Have you met Max?'

'Sort of,' said the Wight, sulkily.

'So you have come to help, too!'

Madame Pinky-Ponky exclaimed. 'I always knew you were good, really, whatever they said about you, all those bad things.'

'Well, I, er … it's, well… Gawd 'elp me, two good deeds in one day,' he muttered under his breath. 'It'll be the end of me, I swear.' After a lot more muttering, he smiled toothily at Madame Pinky-Ponky and turned to the kids. 'OK, yes, I'll help – but it ain't gonner be easy, even with Furry Chops here and Mr Smarty Pants.'

They spent the rest of the morning in the cellar, getting ready. Peregrine gave Svenka a newer version of the Bazooka Blaster she'd used before. 'It's got better missiles than last time – beta bombs:

they're smoke bombs and firecrackers.'

'Thanks!' said Svenka, clearly delighted.

'That net contraption thingy you used on me,' said the Wight, turning to Peregrine, 'rather good. Might build something like it meself – for the spooks. Technology: it's the future, you know!"

'Thanks,' said Peregrine, looking pleased. 'I'm calling it the Belt Utility Module.'

The Wight's lips moved silently, making a B, then a U, and then an M shape and he started to grin.

'Don't even go there,' said Peregrine.

I quite like this Wight, thought Max.

'Well, anyway,' continued the Wight, still trying not to laugh, 'works fine, but that net will be useless. What you need is my Bag O'Spooks. Did you see something glowing deep inside all that gloopy, what-you-call-it ... mummymade?'

'Marmalade,' corrected Peregrine. 'And yes, we all did.'

'Well, that's the spook's spirit – basically all its power 'n' that. Catch that and put it safe in the Bag O'Spooks and we can all go home – 'cept it'll be hard: ghosts like to stay put, that's usually why they haunt a place for hundreds of years. Real homebodies. Our ghost will be settlin' in nicely by now, so it won't like us disturbing it, and it won't be pleased to see me, cos it knows I'll be tryin' to shove it back into a dark, smelly sack.'

'What do you suggest?' asked Max.

'Glad you asked,' said the Wight, who

definitely seemed to like the sound of his own voice. 'When it sees us, it'll scarper with any luck. So as it's running off, trying to avoid being captured, me and this nice young lady will keep it distracted. Then Fangs here,' he pointed at Max, 'will surprise it, grab the glowing spirit ball at the heart of the gooey ghost and you, Brains, will get your BUM ready...'

'Belt Utility Module,' said Peregrine, crossly.

'Yeah, that too. Bag it up. Job done! Except...'

He held a long skinny finger up and Max felt a cold wind run through the cellar. 'Let's just hope it doesn't go on the attack,' the Wight added darkly.

Twenty minutes later, they were crossing the park, walking by the swings with the children playing and the families picnicking or kicking footballs about, as if it was just an ordinary day.

Except it wasn't, thought Max, feeling a bit nervous.

As they got to the old folks' day centre, they saw the windows were all boarded up with thick sheets of metal. Yellow-and-black tape stopped people coming too close and a sign on the pavement read:

CLOSED
FOREVER!

The Wight (or Timmy, as he was sometimes known, apparently) was hiding in Max's rucksack. Luckily, he wasn't too heavy. He now climbed out and looked for a long time at the building.

'It's in there, all right,' he said.

But Max knew that already: his monster senses were fizzing, going off like fireworks in his head. He couldn't wait to burp.

They ducked under the tape and went around the back. As soon as they got out of sight, Max burped.

There was a blue flash and Monster Max stepped forward. He pulled one of the metal sheets from the patio doors with one giant paw and lifted the heavy door off its hinges. He turned to the others.

'Grafter you,' he said with a big, toothy grin.

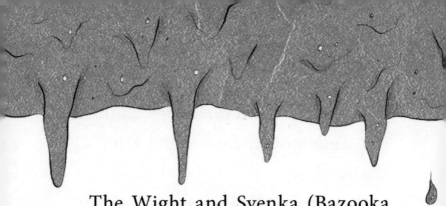

The Wight and Svenka (Bazooka Blaster at the ready) went in first, then Peregrine and finally Monster Max.

Sticky, oozing marmalade covered everything: it hung from curtain rails, just like gloopy ivy, and splodged its way across the ceiling in bulging lumps that dripped down onto the carpet, ever so slowly, like stalactites in a cave. The inside of the day centre now reminded Max of some weird, creepy, orange cavern.

Apart from the steady drip-splat of marmalade, and the TV fuzzing quietly

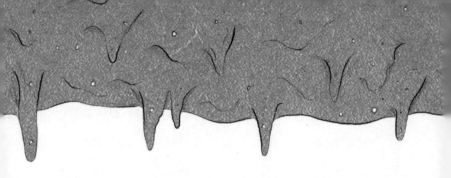

in the corner, there was no sound, and no sign of the ghost anywhere.

'Gris doesn't feel good,' said Max out of the corner of his mouth, as they all tiptoed forward, nerves jangling, hearts beating too fast.

'It knows we're here,' said the Wight. 'It's a clever one. I'm not so sure it will run away.'

'What we do if it decides to be mean?' asked Svenka.

'We fight,' said both Max and Peregrine.

So they edged forward, towards the kitchen, as the atmosphere got creepier.

All the rooms were filled with a dark-orange glow and the smell of ripe oranges. They just needed some sharp, scratchy music and it would have been exactly like a spooky film.

As they got to the swing doors, Max went to the front to protect the others. He took a deep breath and was about to push the doors open, when something shot out of the corridor to their right.

'Aargh!' they all cried.

Monster Max swiped at it with his huge paws but missed. The Wight hit the floor at the same time as Peregrine and as Svenka pulled the trigger of the bazooka, sending a smoke bomb uselessly out of the patio doors into the garden, where it went off with a muffled boof.

They all stared across the room at the pigeon perching on top of the TV.

'Coo?' said the pigeon a little nervously.

'Phew,' said the Wight picking himself up, 'for a second I thought that wa–'

'WHARRGH!'

Before he could finish what he was saying or anyone could get into their planned positions, the kitchen doors burst open and the Marmalade Ghost exploded out with a gloopy roar.

SHOWTIME

Since they had last seen it, the ghost had got way, way bigger and looked quite a lot scarier, too. Its long, sticky claws had grown longer and its mouth was now a huge, gurgling hole, splatting clods of marmalade all over through its tacky teeth, nearly as big as Max's.

Where its heart might have been, deep inside its body, the Spirit Core glowed and throbbed like a ghostly lightbulb.

'WOAHRRRR!' it howled as it

smashed through the kitchen doors and crashed into its old master, the Wight, knocking him over. A dripping, tentacle-like arm shot out sideways and slapped the Bazooka Blaster out of Svenka's hands.

'WOAHRRRRRR WOAHRRRRRR WAAAAHHHHH!'

It made straight for Peregrine, as if it knew he had the Bag O'Spooks that could capture it.

'RAAR!' Max jumped into its path to defend his friend.

Orange hairy monster and orangier sticky poltergeist collided with a giant

Splat!, like a ball of slime the size of a hippo hitting a brick wall. It gave Peregrine time to escape, as Max reached out a giant paw and made a grab for the Spirit Soul.

But the Marmalade Ghost was too quick and wobbled backwards, making a surprised 'waaaaaa' sound as it retreated as fast as it could down the corridor.

Even so, Max almost had his claws on it. The tip of one scraped the glowing Spirit Soul and Max felt a huge blast of spectral energy run through him.

'We've got it on the run!' said the Wight, as Svenka picked up her bazooka again and fired one beta bomb after another into the wobbling shrouds of marmalade, as the ghost fled across the day room.

Peregrine took up a position by a sofa

and pressed a button on his Belt Utility Module, arming the Bag O'Spooks, as Max surged forward with another roar, scattering armchairs and tables, all the time grabbing at the Spirit Soul.

But the Marmalade Ghost went on the attack: a gooey arm like a tentacle shot out and slapped Max between the eyes. The force was enough to shoot him right across the room, and hit the wall in a daze.

The tentacles whipped about, like a gooey sea monster's, smashing into the Wight and Svenka, who both crashed into the large sofa where Peregrine was taking shelter.

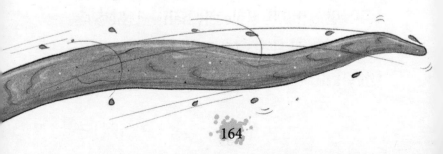

Svenka raised the bazooka to fire, but it had been glooped up in marmalade and wouldn't work.

'Uh ohs,' she said, as Max tried to get up, but he was weak and woozy from being hit in the face.

The ghost opened its mouth very wide. 'WAAAAAARRRRRRRR,' it wailed, 'WAAAARRRRRRRRR!'

Globs of marmalade detached themselves from the ceiling, the furniture and the floor, and joined the main body of the ghost, making it bigger and bigger. Soon it was huge – all spooky teeth and sticky claws coming for the Wight, Svenka and Peregrine, who crouched helplessly behind the sofa.

Max looked on with a horrible feeling they had lost again, worried what the monster might do to his friends.

No, thought Max, shaking his head to clear it. NO!

PROTECT, roared a voice in his head, and Max took a deep breath and burped again and again and again…

RAAAARRRRRR!

Max was bigger, hairier and much, much scarier than he'd ever been in his life.

He bent his thick, shaggy legs and jumped with all his might, smashing through the ceiling of the day centre, through the roof and up, up into the air, going higher than he'd ever gone before in all his monstering. As he got to the top of his jump, so high that dabs of cloud began to appear like tiny puffs of smoke, he looked down at the day centre

– a small patch of red roof far below. Then he dropped at supersonic speed.

Hero-style.

The Marmalade Ghost hadn't noticed any of this, because he was too busy scaring the pants off the Wight, Svenka and Peregrine. In fact, Peregrine had had the pants scared off him so much, all you could see was his BUM sticking out from behind the sofa.

The Marmalade Ghost let out one last ghoulish, gluggy roar and shot forward, its pointy talons, tacky tendrils and sticky teeth stretching out towards Max's three friends, trapped in terror.

Just as Max came roaring down – two whole tons of hairy monster.

'GRET YOUR STICKY CLAWS OFF MY FRIENDS!' he bellowed, bursting

through the roof and landing on the Marmalade Ghost with a tremendous SPLAT, like a meteorite landing in a lake of jelly.

The Marmalade Ghost exploded into thousands of tiny dark-orange droplets, covering Max, Peregrine, Svenka and Timmy (the only partly evil Wight) in thick but strangely delicious goo.

'HA!' cried Max, but he didn't have time to celebrate.

'Get the Spirit Soul,' shouted Timmy frantically, jumping up and down on his bony legs.

Max turned just as the glowing, round ball shot past him. He made a grab for it but missed.

'If it gets outsidet,' Timmy said, 'it'll be harder to catch than ever!'

Svenka picked up the Bazooka Blaster, bashed the side to clean out the marmalade and fired another beta bomb. And missed.

Peregrine pressed and twisted a key on his belt and a mini zinger-net shot out, but too late. The Spirit Soul was going too fast, heading right for the open door.

Just then, a figure appeared outside – a silhouette carrying what looked like … a cricket bat? Until the strange figure moved, it had been hidden by the billowing smoke left by the beta bomb, thanks to Svenka. It was Reg.

As the Spirit Soul shot through the door, well on its way to causing mayhem and madness in the town, they all saw Reg step out of the smoke and swing the cricket bat he was carrying. There

was a loud whack and the Spirit Soul
shot back inside again – now glowing
an angry, frustrated red, corkscrewing
towards Max, who leaped into the air
and kicked it.

It was the worst scissor kick in the history of scissor kicks. If there had been a goal, Max would have missed it by a whole football pitch. Max landed with a loud crash and an OOF!

He looked up. The Spirit Soul had skidded off Max's giant, hairy foot and was now bouncing between the ceiling and the floor like a rubber ball, sending out sparks of spectral energy in all directions.

Peregrine had it in his sights. He ran across the room, his feet making sucky, squelchy noises. He dived (or perhaps tripped) and somersaulted as he pressed a button and his BUM came to the rescue: the Wight's Bag O'Spooks shot out as Peregrine twisted in the air like a nerdy acrobat and…

…scooped up the Marmalade Ghost's Spirit Soul cleanly in the bag.

Instantly, the creepy orange glow disappeared from the room and Max heard the birds outside start to sing.

They trudged home in exhausted, sticky silence, broken only by the sound of flies arriving from all directions, attracted by the smell of marmalade.

'Thanks, Reg,' was all Max (now back to being a boy) had the energy to say as they stumbled past the bins.

'That's fine,' said Reg. 'I heard a commotion and decided to investigate. Glad I brought my cricket bat. I'd have been stumped without it.'

Several wasps had now appeared.

'Let's walk faster,' suggested Svenka.

When they got to Max's house – tired, but happy and very, very relieved – they took their shoes and socks off to stop the floor getting covered in marmalade and went upstairs. Max's parents were out but Madame Pinky-Ponky knew just where the spare towels were kept, because Max definitely didn't.

Max's house has thirteen bathrooms.

Much later, Max's parents came back to find everyone in the kitchen with a mug of chicken soup in one hand and a lump of fluffy, puffy, white bread in the other.

Just one look at the exhausted but pleased faces told them all they needed to know, but Max's dad asked anyway.

'Did you sort the ghost?'

'Yup, you could say...' Max paused and then started to grin.

'Don't say it,' said Peregrine looking up from his mug. 'Please don't.'

'... that it ...' If Max grinned any more, his head was going to fall off.

'Oh, no,' said Timmy.

'It ... it came to a sticky end!'

13

LUCKY

Everyone stayed the night, even Svenka, who phoned her aunt to let her know, and then they all got up (after a nice long lie-in) for a late breakfast of toasted crumpets and hot, buttered rolls. With honey or jam. Absolutely no marmalade.

Max saw Timmy in the corridor by the front door with his Bag O'Spooks. He was talking to Madame Pinky-Ponky. He looked as if he was leaving, so Max went over as Madame Pinky-Ponky turned and walked past Max, blowing her nose.

'Er,' said the Wight, 'I'll be off, then.'

'You can stay for a bit … if you like,' said Max. 'I'm sure my parents won't mind.'

'Nah, you're all right,' the Wight coughed. 'Anyway, Fanghorn will be expecting me back and I've probably got some explaining to do.'

'Won't he be angry? Try and punish you or something?'

''E doesn't scare me. Well, he might, a bit, but he's not completely in charge of Krit … yet. I'll make up some excuse. He'll be mad but he can't eat everyone that upsets him and I don't think I'd be that tasty anyway.'

'OK,' said Max. 'But thanks for everything.'

'Nah, don't mention it.' The Wight coughed again and looked embarrassed. 'I'm not one for goodbyes, so tell the others it's been a blast and I'll be seein' them around, I guess. Bye.'

And with that, the Wight slipped through the half-open front door and was soon lost among the bushes and shadows that lined the neat front gardens down Max's street.

Later, when Max went up to the library to tidy up the books he had scattered everywhere during his long night of research, he saw a bag on the table. It was the same one he'd seen on the Wight's belt. And there was a note.

Max read the note.

And opened the bag.

His mouth dropped open. He grabbed the bag and rushed down the stairs, past his surprised friends and out of the front door.

Max ran all the way across the park, along the edge of the play area with the swings, through the shortcut by the bins and across the road.

When he got to the day centre, he wasn't a bit surprised to see even more barriers and danger signs up and men with machines that looked suspiciously as if they were ready to knock things down.

Mrs Mwangi, Mrs Patel, Mrs Parks, Dottie, Sidney and Reg were all there, standing in a sad group at a safe distance.

Mrs Mwangi saw Max and ran towards him.

At first, Max thought he was in trouble: was she going to wallop him with her massive handbag? But instead she gave him a big hug.

'Brave, brave boy!' she said. 'Reginald has told us everything.'

'Shankfoo,' said Max, who was having difficulty breathing and being hugged by Mrs Mwangi at the same time.

'It's just a shame we're not able to save the day centre,' said Mrs Patel. 'So many years here, so many people all making friends and having somewhere to go. And now no more.'

Through three layers of woolly cardigan, Max heard the sound of feet skidding to a halt. He turned with everyone else to see Peregrine and Svenka panting because they had run across the park too, following Max.

They also got almost hugged to death by Mrs Mwangi.

'Blimey O'Reillys,' said Svenka (who had obviously been spending too much time with Timmy). 'Big mess, this place.'

'Can't argue with that,' said Peregrine.

'So it's being knocked down?' Max asked Reg, pointing at all the big yellow machines.

'I'm afraid so.' Reg shook his head sadly. 'There's no money to rebuild the centre. We'd run out of money before all the spooky stuff started happening, anyway. It was just a matter of time, I suppose.'

'Reg,' said Max, really hoping he was

right about this, 'I think this might help.'

With that, he took the Wight's bag from his pocket and tipped the shining contents into his hand.

Everybody stopped and stared. Really stared. Mrs Patel said something not in English.

Reg, who was closest, seemed to have lost the power of speech. He gasped and shook his head and then he chuckled, before eventually managing to get some words out. 'Well, I'll be...' he said, scratching his head and laughing.

The small pile of rubies and diamonds winked happily in the sun, which had just poked over the tops of the trees. Like hope.

And, at that moment, Max, Peregrine – and everybody else – knew it was all going to be OK.

The note the Wight had left in the bag with the jewels was caught by a sudden gust and it flapped across the grass and plastered itself to a tree.

A gift, from Krit

it said in scrawly writing

I know you will spend it well and I
know we'll be seeing you one day, back in
the Old Country,
cheers Timmy

14

FANGHORN GETS REALLY ANGRY

'What do you mean, they defeated you!'
Fanghorn howled. His eyes flashed red,
flecked with black, like the core of a
dying volcano.

The Wight held his gaze, doing his best to show no fear. 'The boy is getting stronger and his friends are cunning. Best-quality ghouls and ghosts, those were, like I say, but they were no match for Monster Max and this Peregrine Genius.'

'And did you see her?'

'Who?'

'Her!'

'Her who?'

Fanghorn growled, low and deep – less wolf, more T-Rex.

Timmy swallowed hard, wondering if he'd gone too far.

'Oh, *her* her,' he said. 'The princess. Well, no – not as such.' He paused and a cunning looking came over his very wrinkly face. 'She has become very powerful, too,' he said, warming up to a good fib. 'She's a mystery, a myth: magic and mighty. No one sees her properly – only if you're really lucky, you might just catch her shadow racing through the night, silent and sneaky, a fang glinting in the moon, a snarl…'

'Go!' barked Fanghorn, who'd just decided he'd heard enough from this odd, disrespectful creature.

Timmy the Wight nodded. He didn't need to be asked twice. 'Righty-ho. See yer, Puppy-chops!'

Fanghorn leaped forward with a snarl, but was too late. The Wight had already disappeared into the forest.

He frowned. It was obvious that using other creatures from Krit was a waste of time – even if they were scared of him, they were not to be trusted. Fanghorn thought for a while and, as he did so, his frown slowly disappeared and his teeth bared in a terrifying, wolfish grin. He knew what to do.

It was time to send in the wolves…

Want to find out more about Max,

Peregrine and their adventures?

Come to **WWW.MONSTERMAX.CO.UK**

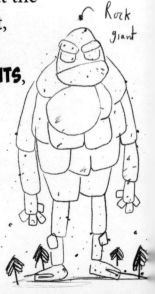

We've **exclusive stories,**

cool videos

and lots more about the
Kritters of Krit,

Rock
giant

like the **ROCK GIANTS,**

the ICE WITCH

Ice Witch.

and the WOLVES...

AND DON'T MISS

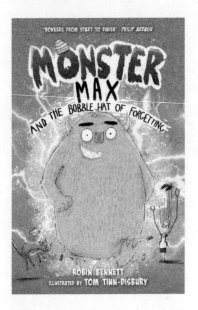

'This is a monsterific romp that had me
howling with laughter. '
Swapna Haddow, author of *Dave Pigeon*

'a funnily monstrous & monstrously funny adventure.'
Gareth P Jones, author of *Dragon Detective* series

'*Monster Max and the Bobble Hat of Forgetting* has mystery,
adventure, and is very, very funny.' **BookTrust**